Transuranic

Start Publishing PD LLC
Copyright © 2024 by Start Publishing PD LLC

Start Publishing PD is a registered trademark of Start Publishing PD LLC
Manufactured in the United States of America

Cover art: Shutterstock/Taisiya Kozorez

Cover design: Jennifer Do

10 9 8 7 6 5 4 3 2 1

ISBN 979-8-8809-2401-1

Transuranic

by Edmond Hamilton

Unexpected Discovery

It was Andersen's queer talk that marked the beginning of it for us. Of course, that wasn't the real beginning. I suppose you might say it really started when Becquerel first puzzled over his fogged photographic plates. But to us, Andersen's premonitions were the start.

We called him the "Melancholy Dane." But that was just a joke, though his tall, cadaverous appearance fitted it. He wasn't really a gloomy sort, and was a first-class nuclear chemist. That was why he surprised us with what he said at dinner that night.

The talk had been shop talk, of course it nearly always was that, at Transuranic Station. Zarias had been triumphant about the way that Element Number 144 was going through the "canyons."

"Fifty new transuranic elements, not counting the gaps!" he exulted. "And I'm sure One-forty-four will be at least semi-stable."

Andersen spoke, then.

"I have a feeling that what we are doing here is against the cosmic scheme," he said in his slow English.

Zarias goggled. He was a fat, bald and irreverent Greek, a brilliant physicist with about as much mysticism as a doorknob.

"Cosmic scheme?" he repeated. "What are you talking about?"

Andersen's sallow face flushed a little as he saw that we were all looking at him curiously.

"I mean," he said hesitantly, "that all these transuranic elements we're creating here are purely man-made. Nothing like them ever existed in the natural cosmos. They're an artificial intrusion, a brand-new order of matter that doesn't rightly belong in our universe at all."

Zarias snorted. "My dear Dane, I'd advise you to consult our friend Varez on the state of your psyche."

I saw that Andersen was a little hurt. "He's only joking, Nils," I put in.

Zarias swore. "I am not joking, Drummond. When a serious scientist starts going mystic, it's time he had his complexes checked."

"Come, come, gentlemen," said Burris, in his mocking way. "We must remember not to get on one another's nerves!"

We all laughed at that, for it was spoken in the Director's pompous manner, and recalled the best joke we had at Transuranic Station. It was a worn-out joke, but still welcome in our isolation and monotony.

Now please don't misunderstand me. I'm not going to strike that "Ah, the loneliness of it all!" pose. The first atomic scientists who served at Transuranic

Transuranic

Station pretty well overdid that pose for the benefit of an admiring world. Personally, it always made me sick.

*

But it *was* a lonely environment; there's no getting away from that. Thirty scientists and technicians, twenty-one of them men and nine of them women, doing a six-month stretch in this complex tomb of concrete and metal sunk in the face of the Moon.

When we had first arrived to take over Transuranic Station, we had been solemnly admonished by Cubbison, our Director.

"The most important thing of all," he told us, "is not to get on one another's nerves."

The joke of that was that Cubbison himself was the only man who got on everybody's nerves. Doctor Walter Cubbison—he always insisted on the "Doctor"—was as fine a specimen of scientific bureaucrat as you'd want to see. He had done good research back in the 1950's but that wasn't what had wangled the Commission on Atomic Energy into making him head of Transuranic Station. It was his political ability, we all knew.

"There must be no emotional obstacles to our work," he had adjured us. "All such problems must be submitted to our able psychologist, Doctor Varez."

Well, despite Cubbison's worry over our nerves, we hadn't had to bother Varez yet. We were too well-adjusted a lot for that. But now Nils Andersen seemed to have gone off the deep end, a little.

He had given me something to think about, though. It had never occurred to me that Transuranic Station was an outpost of unprecedented defiance of normality. But in a way, it was.

It's not easy to explain to laymen. It's all very well to write a "Primer of the Atom," but you just can't make nuclear physics as easy to understand as a ball game. But I'll try to explain what Andersen meant.

There were, until the early 1940's, ninety-two elements in nature. They ran from hydrogen up to uranium, from atomic Number One to Ninety-two. Those elements made up everything in nature. Mendelieff had neatly arranged them in his periodic table and there just weren't any more.

Then they got to bombarding uranium with neutrons to create the uranium fission on which atomic energy is based. And they found that one isotope of uranium would absorb a neutron and then eject an electron. That stepped up its atomic number, the number of charges in its nucleus, from ninety-two to ninety-three. And that meant it wasn't uranium any longer but a brand-new element, neptunium.

Neptunium was boosted up naturally by the same process to atomic Number Ninety-four, and so we had plutonium. And then in 1946 the University of California scientists started the job of trying to add carbon, Number Six, to uranium, to make another new element—Number Ninety-eight.

You see what had happened? For the first time in history, the "normal" range of ninety-two elements had been extended. New elements, transuranic elements, had been created such as had never appeared at all naturally. They were a totally artificial new kind of matter.

Of course, the atomic physicists didn't stop there. They kept up the boosting process to create more new transuranic elements. By 1960 they had run the transuranic elements clear up to Number One-twenty-eight. Of course, many of them were unstable and could be kept in existence only under special conditions. And after the Cambridge disaster, the Commission got a little nervous about the whole business.

That's why they had established Transuranic Station up here on the Moon where a blow-up wouldn't harm anybody—except scientists. The rocket boys had got to the Moon before 1951 and had found it wasn't good for much else but such a station. So it had been built here on the face of the flat Mare Imbrium.

The "Dome" was what we called the central living quarters. For safety in emergency it had forty-foot walls that could stop any radiation ever heard of. The labs were grouped loosely around it like planets around a sun, connected by sealed underground tunnels. The big atomic piles and separation "canyons" ran off underground, with full remote-control facilities.

The whole place was Earth-conditioned, with magnetized floors that approximated normal gravity when we wore our steel-soled shoes. Even so, men and women couldn't take more than six months of it without organic trouble. We were the second shift of scientists to work at the Station.

*

We had begun where the first shift left off, at transuranic element Number One-thirty-six. And with Zarias sparking the work, we had run the new elements up to a hundred and forty-four, the last one just being separated now. And it looked as though we're now working into a more stable series of elements.

Transuranic

That's why Andersen irked me a little with his talk of these new elements being a challenge to the normal cosmos.

"Everything man does is a challenge like that," I told him next day in his lab. "The first time he smelted iron or sent a radio message, it was the same."

Andersen shook his head. "Not quite the same, Drummond. Iron and electromagnetic vibrations always existed in Nature. We just used them. But these transuranic elements—they *never* existed before."

Before I could argue further, the inter-phone across his lab squawked in Zarias' voice.

"Drummond! Andersen! Come over here and I'll show you something!"

We went through the tunnels in a hurry, to Main Physics lab. There were already a half-dozen others there—Marie Laurent, Burris, Varez and others.

"Take a look at the panel of Chamber N!" Zarias yelled at us.

The remote-controls that handled all the machinery in the "canyons" and buried chambers outside the labs were concentrated on one wall of Main Physics lab. There was a panel of registering gauges and a televisor screen above the controls of each distant chamber.

We looked in the screen first. In Chamber N was a roughly oval mass of tawny metal that was a foot across.

"Element One-forty-four, huh?" I said to Zarias. "You've sure separated a lot of it."

"Look at those radiation gauges!" he yelped. "The gauges, not the screen!"

We looked, and were stunned. The gauges showed that radiation was pouring out *through* the walls of Chamber N.

"Holy cats!" yelled Burris. "Chamber N is leaking radiation like a sieve!"

"Impossible!" exclaimed Marie Laurent, blue eyes stunned. "Those walls should hold everything from Alpha to neutrons! Let me check it!"

When she and Burris, our two radiation experts, finished that check, they looked more dazed than before. Marie wiped back a disorderly lock of her heavy dull-blond hair, in a stunned way.

"That radiation from Element One-forty-four is something completely new!" she said incredulously. "It's way down in the forty-fourth minus octave, and it's going through those ray-proof walls like paper!"

Zarias began to swear. He swore in Greek, and he hardly ever did that. I knew then how badly upset he was.

"We've stumbled onto something new, and maybe it's bad and maybe it's good, but it's new!" he finished. "A new type of radiation!"

All this time, Andersen had stood behind me staring into the visor of Chamber N in a blank sort of way. In our excitement, we hadn't paid him any attention. But now as we stood dazed and silent, he spoke. He spoke in a queer, halting way, his eyes fixed on the televisor screen.

"We must bring that mass of One-forty-four and a lot of the other transuranic elements out of the chambers, into this lab," he said.

Burris uttered a yelp. "Are you crazy? That new ray might induce enough unpredictable activity in the other elements to trigger a big fission!"

Andersen just looked at him vaguely. "We must do that," he murmured. "It has been born, but It is still weak. We must help It grow stronger, or It will die."

There was a sick silence, then. And in it, all the excitement of our unexpected discovery drained right out of us.

An Alien Intrusion

We knew what had happened, all right. It happened to three of the first shift of scientists at Transuranic Station. They had cracked up badly, and that's why we had a psychologist with our shift.

I realized now we should have known it the way Andersen had talked the night before. Of course, he had seemed normal then. But now his dazed, earnest look and halting, crazy talk meant just one thing.

Varez went to him and spoke quietly. "Perhaps you are right, Nils. Will you come and talk it over with me?"

Andersen looked at him earnestly. "You understand, Ramon? It needs strength. We must help It."

"I understand a little," said Varez, taking the Dane's arm. He walked with him toward the door. "I want you to explain it to me."

And then Varez' good work was nearly undone by Doctor Cubbison. He stood in the door, and his high, rasping voice complained.

"Really, Doctor Andersen, I am surprised at your absurd suggestion! I really feel I must report this to the Commission."

"That will be enough," said Varez in his soft voice, and yet there was something in it that shut Cubbison up at once.

But when Varez and Andersen had gone, Cubbison started again.

"This new radiation must be shielded off at once!" he fussed. "See to it

Transuranic

immediately, Doctor Laurent! I'll report to New York."

It was like him, that order. It was like him to order Marie to devise instantly a shield for a radiation that no one before had dreamed to exist. But she silently started making capture cross-section tests of various shielding materials, by the remote-control.

By that "evening"—we kept Earth time at the Station—the radiation from Element One-forty-four was still a mystery. It was still leaking out of that chamber, though of course even it couldn't enter the Dome. Marie and Burris had been making their capture cross-sections all day.

Zarias was badly upset, at dinner that night in the Dome. He was upset because this new radiation had suddenly cut the ground from under all the physics he knew so well.

"We're exactly where the Curies and Rutherford were fifty years ago!" he kept saying. "We're on the brink of unexplored territory!"

Marie Laurent was silent at dinner, and afterward I saw her go up the stair to the lookout. I followed and found her gazing out of the filter-windows at the glaring, ghastly desert of the Mare Imbrium over which swung the dull green shield of Earth.

They say that when a man reports for duty at Transuranic Station he spends his whole first day peering raptly from the lookout, and then never goes up there again. It's nearly the truth—the novelty of being on the Moon wears off fast, when nothing out there ever changes.

Marie turned around and smiled at me. "You might have waited long enough to make your coming look casual, Frank."

"Why the devil should I?" I told her. "Everyone in the Station knows how I chase you."

She didn't object when I kissed her. I liked the cool firmness of her lips, and the warm firmness of her body in my arms, and the way her disorderly lock of dull-blond hair fell across her forehead.

She wasn't pretty. Her mouth was too wide and her face had a little too much strength. No, she wasn't pretty—but she was beautiful.

She pushed me away. "I'm getting to like that a little too much, Frank."

"I wish you'd take me seriously," I complained.

She laughed. "Be reasonable! I'm twenty-nine years old to your twenty-seven, I'm a very plain girl, and we don't know each other at all. It's just propinquity."

Edmond Hamilton

I was annoyed because she always fended me off that way. But before I could argue, we heard a step on the stair. It was Varez who came up into the lookout. He smiled at us in his quiet way. He was a dark, soft-spoken young Costa Rican whom we all liked.

"Just the man I want to see," I said. "I have an emotional problem. It's Marie."

"What can I do about that, Drummond?" he countered.

Marie laughed. "Probably Frank wants you to order me to spend a week-end with him, when we return to Earth."

"You French all have evil minds," I told her. And then asked Varez, "Tell her she has to marry me."

Varez laughed softly. "Transuranic Station is like heaven in only one way—there is no giving in marriage. I can't help you, Drummond."

*

It struck me suddenly that he looked tired and depressed.

"What about Nils?" I asked. "Is he all right now?"

"I don't know," murmured the psychologist.

He peered out of the window at the terminator creeping like a tide of darkness across the ghastly lunar plain. In the Earthshine, distant craters fanged the star-specked sky.

"Can you tell us what Andersen meant by his talk in the lab?" Marie asked him soberly.

Varez turned slowly. "It's all rather baffling. He talked at first only of something called 'It'. It had been born and It must grow. It needed strength."

He frowned. "When I tried to probe deeper, I just couldn't get anywhere. I tried hypnosis, but it didn't work. That amazed me, for Andersen seemed a susceptible type. I finally gave him a sedative and left him to sleep."

Marie was silent a moment. "Do you think there could be any connection—"

She was interrupted by feet pounding up the little steel stair. It was Carew, the gangling English youngster who was Zarias' assistant, who burst into the lookout. He looked upset.

"Doctor Varez, I thought I ought to tell you! I just saw Doctor Andersen going into Main Physics lab! Of course it's none of my business, but I heard about what happened today, and he looked so queer and dazed!"

All three of us were startled.

"We'd better get hold of him at once!" exclaimed Varez.

11

Transuranic

We ran down the stair, and Burris and Mathers, the chief mathematician of the Station, joined us as we hurried across the Dome to the main tunnel into the labs. Burris' face was taut as he ran.

"That cracked idea of his of bringing a lot of the transuranic elements together—if he tried that—"

"This way!" yelled Zarias, his voice from ahead of us sounding strangled. "Hurry!"

We burst into the big Main Physics lab. The first thing we saw was Zarias scrambling to his feet by one wall. His face was deathly white and he had blood on his forehead.

Across the big lab, Andersen was working like a madman with the remote-controls by which the transuranic elements could be mechanically brought from their safety chambers into the lab. The Dane had a blank, unseeing look on his face as he yanked conveyor-switches one after another.

Burris yelled as we ran forward. I heard the clash and grind of gears, and glimpsed lead trays sliding out of their conveyor tubes onto the racks, trays with a dozen different new transuranic elements in them.

The tray with the oval mass of Element One-forty-four in it popped out, as I ran forward. Instantly, that ovoid of tawny metal burst into a shimmering glow of light that seemed to reach toward the other trays.

Zarias shouted thickly behind me. "Stop him before he brings—"

I have to choose my words carefully now. For what happened in the next instant is still not too clear in my memory. There was a sudden feeling of tension in the air. It was the hunch, the sixth sense, that thrills through a radiologist sometimes just before a blow-up.

"Look *out*!" Burris yelled, and I knew from that that he felt it, too.

And then it hit us. I'm not trying to be cryptic about all this. It's just that it was so unearthly it's hard to describe. There was a feeling of tingling force going through my body, and at the same moment something jabbed into my mind. I mean that I felt an alien intrusion battering into my thoughts.

I want to be precise. And I know that what I've just written may recall fantasies of alien beings delicately and deftly probing into the human mind. It wasn't like that at all. The nearest I can describe it is this way—if my mind were a complicated watch, what had grabbed it was the uncertain, fumbling hand of a child.

"Frank!" said Marie uncertainly, her face drained of all color. And then she suddenly screamed it. "*Frank!*"

Edmond Hamilton

*

Burris was the one who saved us then. He said afterward that he felt that sickening, fumbling mental grasp as we did, but that his first premonition of a blow-up had given him a certain physical momentum that carried him through.

Anyway, he was the one who shoved us toward the door into the corridor. I don't remember much of that moment. I dimly recall seeing Mathers, his ascetic face blank and strange, walking stiffly toward Andersen as the Dane stood working the chamber-controls.

I don't remember any more of it until the moment I found myself out in the corridor with Zarias and Marie and Varez and young Carew, and heard Burris frantically slamming the Main Physics door. The grabbling of impossible fingers on my brain stopped then. I turned around shakily and found young Carew being sick against the corridor wall.

"What is it?" cried Marie, her eyes wide with horror. "Something that touched our minds, that radiation—"

Zarias saved us from collapse in that moment, I think. The Greek's black eyes were blazing with scientific passion now.

"Andersen was right—he sensed it from the first!" he cried. "It has been born—a new and undreamed of form of life! Transuranic life!"

"You're mad!" Marie said huskily. "It can only be a queer psychological effect of that new radiation!"

"That new radiation *is* life!" Zarias cried fiercely. "Life of a kind never before existing in the cosmos, because the transuranic elements themselves never existed!" He swept on, as we stood dazed. "What is *our* kind of life? Is it the sulfur, phosphorus, and carbon and other elements of our bodies? You know it is not. There's a spark there, a chemical spark kindled long ago on the primal Earth, that unites those inert elements into a living organism.

"The same way with It. This new radiation from Element One-forty-four is the spark—a spark never existing before in the universe. A spark that has grown with superhuman swiftness now, linking separated transuranic elements together in a strange, loose physical body whose nerves are intangible radiation! A body—and a *mind*! Only a newborn mind yet, but powerful enough already to warp Andersen into helping Its body grow in strength by bringing those elements together! And now—"

Zarias didn't get a chance to finish. Carew, sick and staggering, uttered a thin,

Transuranic

high cry.

"It's here again!" His face was ghastly.

My own face must have been, for I felt it, too, at that moment. The fumbling groping of tingling, intangible hands on my brain.

"The Dome!" Zarias shouted thickly. "It's strong enough to reach out of the labs, but the Dome's walls will hold It out!"

Clutching Fingers

As we stumbled frantically down the corridor, my arm was around Marie. Zarias yanked an alarm signal as he ran, and bells shrilled up and down the corridors. Feet pounded down the lab tunnels, and startled voices called questions.

That general alarm jammed us all at the door of the Dome for a moment. Impossible fingers were fumbling our brains and we were driven by a primitive, unreasoning horror.

Then the ponderous boom of the main door closing punctuated the nightmare experience. I found myself in the little crowd by the door. Nearly everyone in the Station was there, excited and stunned.

Doctor Cubbison appeared on the scene. "What's the reason for the general alarm? Has there been a blow-up?"

Zarias laughed mirthlessly. "There has been a blow-up. A bad one. New life has been born—*new* life. Something alien to our cosmos, something Nature never intended to exist here, but which we clever little people brought into being. Andersen was right last night!" His voice rasped higher. "Right now, It's in there in Main Physics lab! What is It? It's twenty-odd chunks of transuranic elements, formed into an organized body by linking radiation-nerves, by which it can think, feel and *act*. It's only newly born, It doesn't know much yet, but It knows that It wants to grow!"

Cubbison looked impatient. "Really, these dramatics—"

Zarias suddenly relaxed. "You're right. Just dramatics." He looked around. "We're scientists. We have a problem to deal with. And we've got to deal with it quickly before it finishes us."

"What real danger can there be?" Cubbison asked dubiously.

"You didn't feel those fingers of radiation groping at your mind?" Marie asked him.

Burris came stumbling back from across the Dome.

Edmond Hamilton

"I've checked the main telltale panel!" he said hoarsely. "All the canyons are going full tilt. Andersen must be operating them!"

Zarias spoke swiftly and coolly now. "The thing has been born and It wants to grow. And It will grow, using Andersen and Mathers and anyone else It can get hold of to create more transuranic elements, form them into a bigger and bigger body, until Its radiation-mind can reach even through the Dome's walls, even maybe to other worlds!"

I felt the full impact of horror, then. I realized that we had set the stage for the birth of a life of radiation and radiating elements that could not share the cosmos with our own kind of life.

"It can grow colossal, but It isn't colossal now," Zarias went on. "It's newborn, fumbling, groping. We have to kill It before It gets bigger."

"But how?" cried Marie. "How can you kill a thing of chemical elements and radiation?"

The Greek set his teeth. "We've got to get back into Main Physics lab and break up Its body by switching those elements back to their chambers. Then we can use the emergency-charges to explode the chambers and so destroy It."

He looked at Marie and Burris. "We'll need shields to keep that radiation off our brains. What will hold it out best?"

"Beryllium, I think," Burris answered. "It seems to be the foot of beryllium in the Dome's walls that's shielding it out now. But you can't make protective helmets of foot-thick beryllium."

"We'll plate anti-rad helmets as thickly with beryllium as we can," Zarias retorted, "and take our chances."

Cubbison finally got a chance to speak. He spoke as fussily as though all this were some annoying ordinary accident.

"This is all very upsetting! I shall have to report to New York at once. In the mean-time, I leave you in charge of the problem, Doctor Zarias."

He hurried off, and Burris laughed sourly.

"If the universe was about to come to an end, he'd get in a report to New York."

We left Marie to watch the telltales and report to us what Andersen and Mathers were doing in the lab. It was a hideous thing to have in our thoughts as we worked on the helmets—the knowledge that those two were puppets working in the uncanny Thing's grip.

The whole Station was seething with excitement, of course. Everyone swarmed

15

around the improvised workshop where we and the technics sweated to cover three anti-rad helmets with extra-thick layers of beryllium.

*

Everyone knew there had been some kind of a blow-up in Main Physics, but the truth was still too incredible for them. The idea of a new birth of transuranic life, a thing of radiation and unearthly new elements that was a sudden terrible enemy in our midst, was too much for them yet. They thought it was just a crack-up on Andersen's part.

"They may protect us long enough to get at the chamber-controls in there," Zarias muttered, eyeing our clumsy helmets when we finished.

Cubbison came stalking back to us as we returned to the lab corridor entrance. His spectacles glittered worriedly at us.

"I've talked to New York and have arranged with the Commission against any mishap here," he announced.

"What do you mean, mishap?" snapped Zarias. "We've already had one."

"I mean, if we can't cope with this transuranic Thing," Cubbison answered fussily. "It might get all of us under control as it has Andersen and Mathers. In that case, we'd all be working to help It grow. The Commission is sending two rockets at once to take off all Station personnel if the situation here becomes untenable. But in case we're overpowered by the Thing before the rockets can get here, and fail to maintain intelligent communication by televisor, the rockets will drop plutonium bombs on the Station."

We stared at him. "You mean, destroy the Station?" said Burris. "Destroy all of us?"

Cubbison nodded, frowning. "It's regrettable, but it would have to be done if the Thing in there proves too much for us before the rockets come. We can take no chance of Its growing beyond the Moon in power."

Zarias' face worked, and he went up to Cubbison and took his hand. "I want to say that I am sorry, sir," the Greek said huskily.

"Sorry?" Cubbison asked annoyedly. "Sorry about what? Really, Doctor Zarias, you are being obscure."

But we knew what Zarias meant—we all knew, for we all felt the same shame as he did at our misjudgment of the man before us. Pompous, vain, stuffy—yes, Cubbison was all those things. But what we hadn't suspected was that he was the best scientist, and the best man, among us.

16

Edmond Hamilton

We knew, now! We knew it wasn't bureaucratic intriguing that had led the Commission to put him at the head of the Station. We knew, and were ashamed.

I don't think Cubbison dreamed what we were thinking.

"Now, Doctor Zarias," he went on briskly, "if you'll explain how you propose to deal with this Thing?"

"We've got to rush It before It gets stronger," Zarias said. "Burris, Drummond and I will wear these beryllium-shielded helmets. They may hold out the radiation well enough to let us shove the transuranic elements back to their chambers, and thus break Its body up."

"And if the helmets don't hold?" Marie asked anxiously.

No one answered her. There wasn't any answer.

Young Carew stood ready at the lab corridor door as we put on the helmets and adjusted them so we could see through the lead-glass eye-slits. Then we crouched at the door like sprinters before a start.

My heart was hammering and I'm not ashamed to confess that I was horribly afraid. Whatever It was that was in Main Physics, It wasn't anything a man had ever faced before. And if we failed—

Carew gave me no more time to think of that. He swung the heavy door open, we dashed through, and it slammed behind us. We ran down the corridor to Main Physics, and a wild elation soared in me, for aside from a tingling sensation all through me, I didn't feel anything unusual.

"The Thing isn't attacking us!" Burris shouted, muffledly. "We'll make it!"

Whether it was his shout or the fact that we burst into Main Physics lab at that moment that did it, I don't know. I don't, in fact, remember much of the next few minutes. I do recall that as we burst into the lab, Mathers and Andersen were working in the same dazed, mechanical way with the canyon controls.

And I recall that they had arranged the lead trays that contained chunks or heaps of the glowing transuranic elements in a curious circular pattern around the conveyor-rack on which the tray of radiant Element One-forty-four still rested. And that between the One-forty-four and the other elements, the shimmering radiation of Its nerves pulsed and throbbed.

"One-forty-four is the brain—switch it back first!" Zarias shouted as we plunged into the lab.

And then it hit us. It wasn't the groping fingers of radiation that had fumbled with our brains the first time. They were stronger now, those intangible fingers, and they weren't groping.

They grabbed our minds and held them. I was still conscious, I was still Frank Drummond, but I didn't have a body any more. It held my brain and body. I felt the impact of Its mind. And there was no hate or fear or passion in it. There was only—wonder.

It had picked up us three men, had picked us up by our brains just as a child might pick up puppies by their necks and wonderingly examine them. And there was a strange and alien cleanness about that intangible grasp on my brain. It was as clean and strange as starlight.

I knew we had failed, and the part of me that was still Frank Drummond agonized in the knowledge. Then came the crash.

Burris had pitched forward so madly into the lab that he caromed into the blank-faced Mathers, even after It gripped us.

The grip on my brain suddenly relaxed. The crash had startled It, or had turned Its attention for a moment.

"Back out, Drummond!" Zarias screeched.

He clawed me back through the lab door and slammed it. Instantly, the clutch of It grabbed at my brain again. But through that heavy door, through our helmets, the clutch was not quite so strong. We could fight it, out here in the corridor.

"Burris!" I choked, but the Greek gave me a furious shove back down the corridor toward the Dome.

"No use! He's gone! Another second and we'll be gone too!"

Destructive "Toy"

I believe we would not have got into the Dome if Carew had not heard us coming and had the door open in time. The slam of the heavier Dome door cut that unholy, wondering, alien grasp from our minds instantly.

I stumbled and would have fallen but for Marie's firm arm around me. Zarias' face was livid when he took his helmet off, and I knew then what my own must look like.

"Burris?" said Ramon Varez quietly.

"In there," croaked the Greek. "In there working for It now, with Mathers and Andersen. Soon, maybe, all of us will be!" He got a grip on himself and stopped that. "By heaven, no! No Thing of minerals and rays can conquer men! We'll find a way!"

Edmond Hamilton

"The helmets failed, then?" said Cubbison anxiously.

"Too thin," Zarias nodded. "It'll take a foot of beryllium to protect us. That means armor that we can wear into the lab. And we'll have to make it fast."

The Greek was indomitable. In the hours that followed, he sweated with the others as every working facility we had in the Dome was turned to the all-important task of making the foot-thick armor. Beryllium is light, but even so the suits would be heavy and massive. But we wouldn't have to wear them far, if we succeeded.

I'd like to be able to say that I worked as hard as Zarias. I didn't. I was too sick and shaky, for the next hours. Only shame finally made me conquer that and plunge at the job with the others.

"I'll go in this time, and perhaps Carew and Blauner will go with me," Ramon Varez proposed.

Zarias choked him off. "No! Drummond and I go again, and we will kill the Thing this time or not come out!"

I am eternally grateful to him for that. For until then, I had felt I dared not face It again. And after that, I knew I had to.

The hours went by. Our Earth-time schedule was forgotten. We had, to spur us on, Marie's report from the telltales that It must be growing steadily, since the canyons were working ceaselessly to build bigger the transuranic elements that were Its body.

The armor was finished, crude, massive and gleaming. Zarias told Varez and me his plan.

"We will all three try to do the same thing—switch that tray of Element One-forty-four back to its chamber, and blow the chamber. One-forty-four is the brain-center, the life-center, of It. It's the one vulnerable spot."

Marie interrupted with a cry that had so much horror in it that we swung sharply around to where she stood at the telltales. She pointed at the gauges.

"Look! Radiation is filtering into the Dome now!"

We looked. It was true. The new radiation, the radiation that was Its nerve-force and will, was showing on the gauges. And at the same moment we felt, faintly, the strange tingle of that radiation through our bodies.

"If It's filtering through even the Dome's walls," Carew faltered, "then It's so strong now—"

"So strong that our foot-thick beryllium armor is no more good than paper!" I finished hoarsely.

Transuranic

We knew what had happened. Hours before, the armor would have been effective. But in those hours, as we had worked, It had been growing bigger and stronger. Now It was too strong for armor of any kind. Soon It would be too strong even for the massive walls of the Dome.

"We're sunk," said Carew, and sat down heavily and put his face in his hands.

Cubbison's thin shoulders sagged a little. "I fear the situation is bad. Before the rockets can get here to take us off, It will control everyone in the Dome. And when that happens—"

When that happened, when we were all mindless puppets who couldn't answer the televisor, those rockets would carry out Cubbison's orders and obliterate us and the Station together.

"*I* won't quit without at least a fight!" Zarias raged. "I'm going in there!"

*

He started to get into his armor. But Ramon Varez caught his arm.

"Zarias, wait!" cried the Costa Rican. "There's still a chance, if you'll let me try it! A stratagem based on psychology."

Zarias laughed mirthlessly. "Our sciences are our master passions right to death. Thanks, Ramon. But your psychology is no good against a Thing that doesn't live and think as we do."

"Some basic rules of psychology are the same for *any* kind of life!" Varez insisted. "Let me try! It'll take only a few minutes!"

He ran off across the Dome. We didn't look after him. We looked dully and tiredly at each other.

Marie came to me and stood close beside me. What was in her eyes should have made me feel happier, but it didn't. It agonized me to think what we two were going to lose.

Varez came running back. With him, he had a portable ray-projector, one of the compact boxes that can emit radiations of any type and are used to check protective shielding.

"When we burst into the lab," he said eagerly, "I'll use this thing to shoot quick spurts of every kind of radiation, in succession, right at It."

"And what good will that do?" cried Zarias. "Those weak test-rays will never harm It!"

"Give me the chance to try my plan!" pleaded Varez. "There's nothing to be lost. I'll go in there with you, and while I use this thing on It, you and Drummond can try to shove Element One-forty-four back to its chamber."

The Greek shrugged heavily. "I was going in anyway. You can bring your crazy gadget if you like."

I got into my armor without looking at Marie. I knew I wouldn't go into the labs if I looked at her.

Varez and Zarias were in their own armor. Varez held the ray-projector in one jointed beryllium arm. Zarias made a clumsy signal.

"All right!" his muffled voice boomed.

Carew flung the door open, and then we three were through it and clanking down the corridor.

And Its radiation hit us in a mighty blast as we reached the door of Main Physics. It had grown, yes—and now Its radiant will froze us in our tracks.

I felt again that clean, alien grip on my mind and knew I'd never get free of it. I saw Mathers and Anderson and Burris sweating over the canyon controls that kept building It bigger, and knew I'd be sweating with them till a plutonium bomb gave me release.

And then, unexpectedly, the grip of It on our minds incredibly relaxed. I felt Its mental grasp shift from wonder to interest to pure delight. Delight in the thing that Varez held, the box that was spurting an unseen kaleidoscope of rays in an ever-changing pattern! In that, for the moment, Its attention was wholly absorbed.

"*Now!*" yelled Zarias, and we two hurled ourselves forward across the lab.

My hand hit the switch of Chamber N's conveyor. There was a grind of gears, and the tray of Element One-forty-four started sliding swiftly back from its rack into the tube.

Wonder, delight, all the emotions of Its mind changed instantly to alarm! I felt Its thought, as a sudden wave of *hurt* fear. And then it was weakening, fading, as the element that was the brain-center of Its strange life slid back out of the pattern of its unearthly body, back to its distant, buried chamber.

"*Blow it!*" shrilled Varez, and Zarias' hand fumbled for another switch and closed it.

There was a dull, distant roar and the whole Station shook as the tonite explosive charge set under each chamber in case of emergencies blew Chamber N and the Element One-forty-four in it to fragments.

And then there was just a silence in the laboratory, in which I was conscious of Andersen and Burris lying senseless on the floor, and Mathers standing and looking down stupidly at his hands. The tingling force was gone, the impact of Its mind was gone, the shimmering glow of its radiation-nerves was gone. There was nothing here but a pattern of trays of transuranic elements, a pattern that had been a strange living body but that was now a dead one.

*

I felt the others crowding into the lab and helping me out of my armor. Marie was crying as she clung to me.

"How did you do it?" Cubbison was asking Varez over and over again.

Varez looked down at the little ray-projector. "This did it. To It, this was a delightful toy, a toy of radiation, calculated to catch the interest of a creature whose life was radiation, just as a kitten would catch a human child's interest. Psychology—some of its rules are basic. For though It was transuranic, unhuman, non-normal, yet even so it was also very young, and could be distracted by the right kind of toy just as a young child can be. That moment of distraction gave us our chance."

Cubbison beamed. "You've saved the Station, you three! I'll report to New York at once. We shall be careful in future to avoid repetition of this danger. But Transuranic Station's work can go on, thanks to your heroism."

Zarias laughed. He laughed, but we saw now that there were tears in his eyes and running down his cheeks.

"We are heroes, yes," he said. "We are heroes, because we have killed a baby."

His voice lashed bitterly. "For It was just a baby, a baby trying to live and grow up in a wholly alien and hostile world. And we did it to death! Curse all of us for it! What are we but a lot of mucky little apes, strutting around now because we murdered something that could have been bigger than ourselves? It wasn't human, it wasn't of our cosmos, but it was clean and passionless and shining, and it might have made this whole universe one vast and wonderful mind and body! But it wasn't human so we had to kill it—we heroes!"

He put his face in his hands and sat down blindly in a corner.

Varez looked at him. "He was too many times under Its influence," he murmured. "He'll get over it. I—I think I know how he feels."

I thought I knew, too. That burst of wonder and delight at Varez' "toy," that hurt, bewildered grief of the last moment—they were shaking me, too.

Maybe Zarias was right. Maybe we had killed something that could have been bigger and finer than humanity. But still, this isn't a transuranic universe. It was the

Edmond Hamilton

stranger here, not we.

And, I have thought since, maybe it was only a forerunner. Beyond our old range of elements, the potentialities of the transuranic realms still beckon man to create. Perhaps, someday, another It will be born thus which will not die, but will live on after man's day is finished, as his strange successor and son.

www.ingramcontent.com/pod-product-compliance
Lightning Source LLC
Chambersburg PA
CBHW021006150626
46549CB00012BA/1384